WILDSIDE PRESS PRESENTS

I0531003

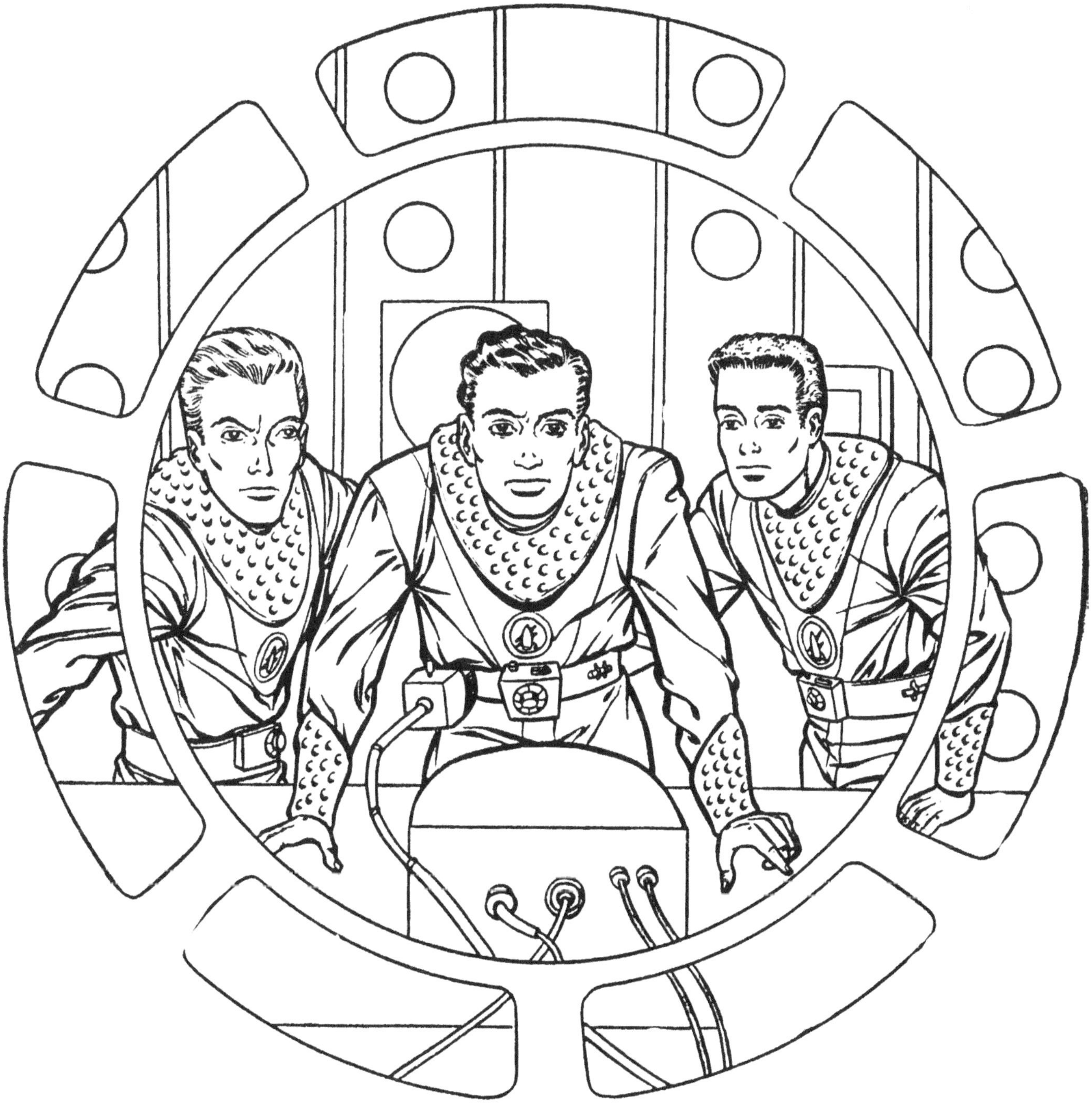

TOM CORBETT SPACE CADET

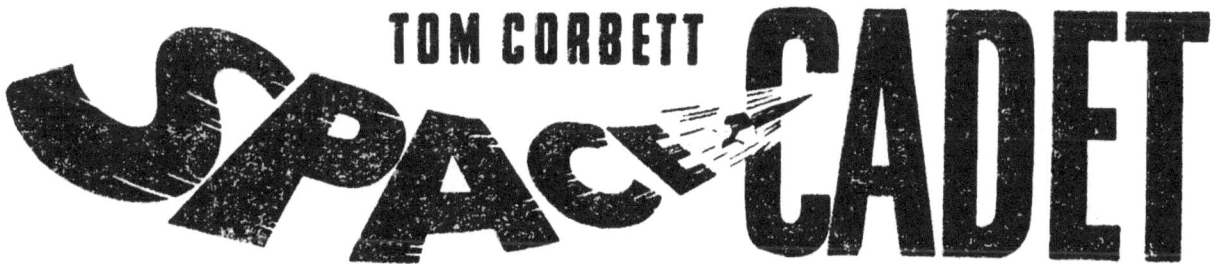

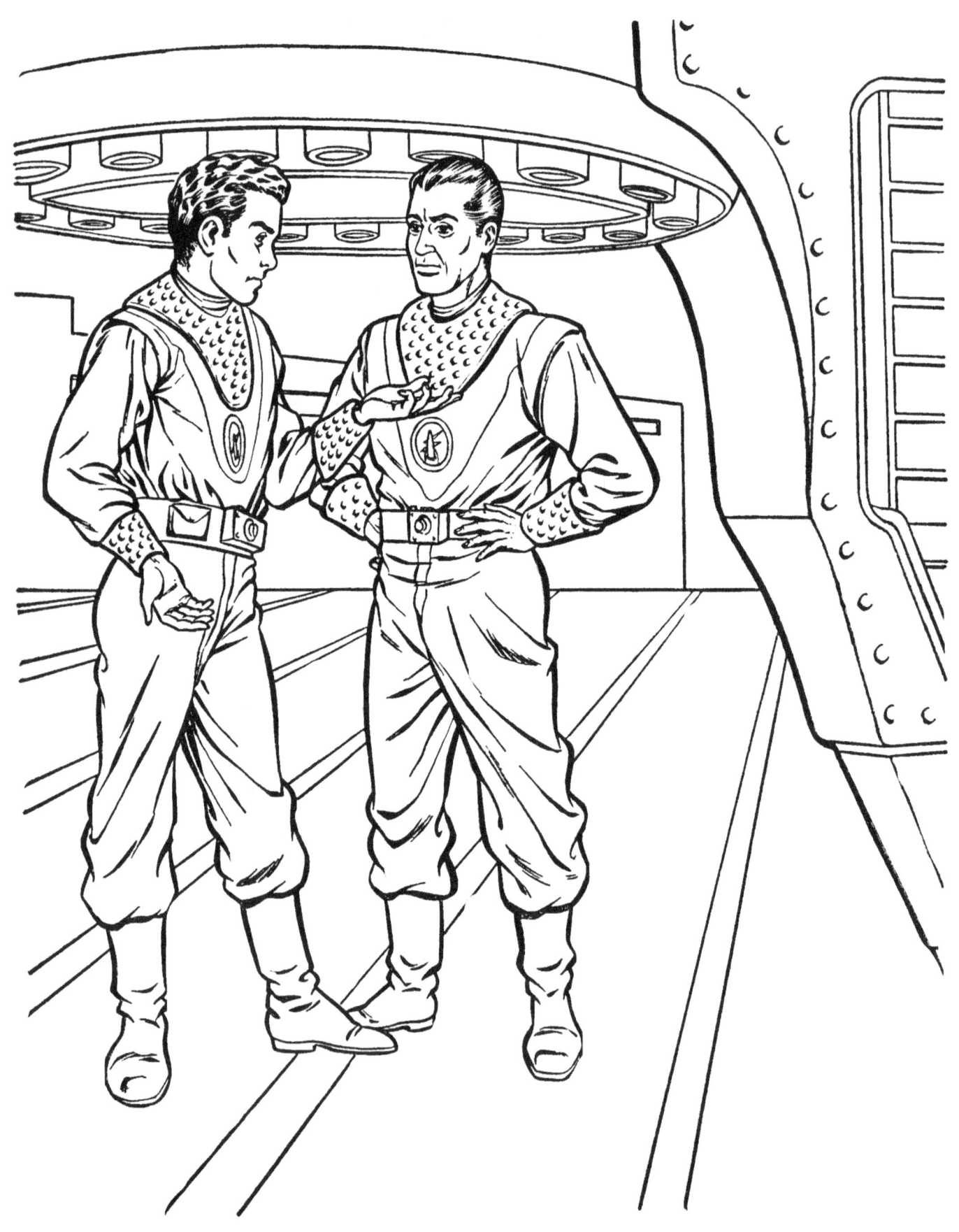

Tom and Commander Arkwright discuss proposed flight

Commander Arkwright and Captain Strong making plans

FLIGHT BRIEFING

FUELING UP

BOARDING TO RAISE SHIP

EMERGENCY CHANGE IN COURSE

THE BLAST-OFF

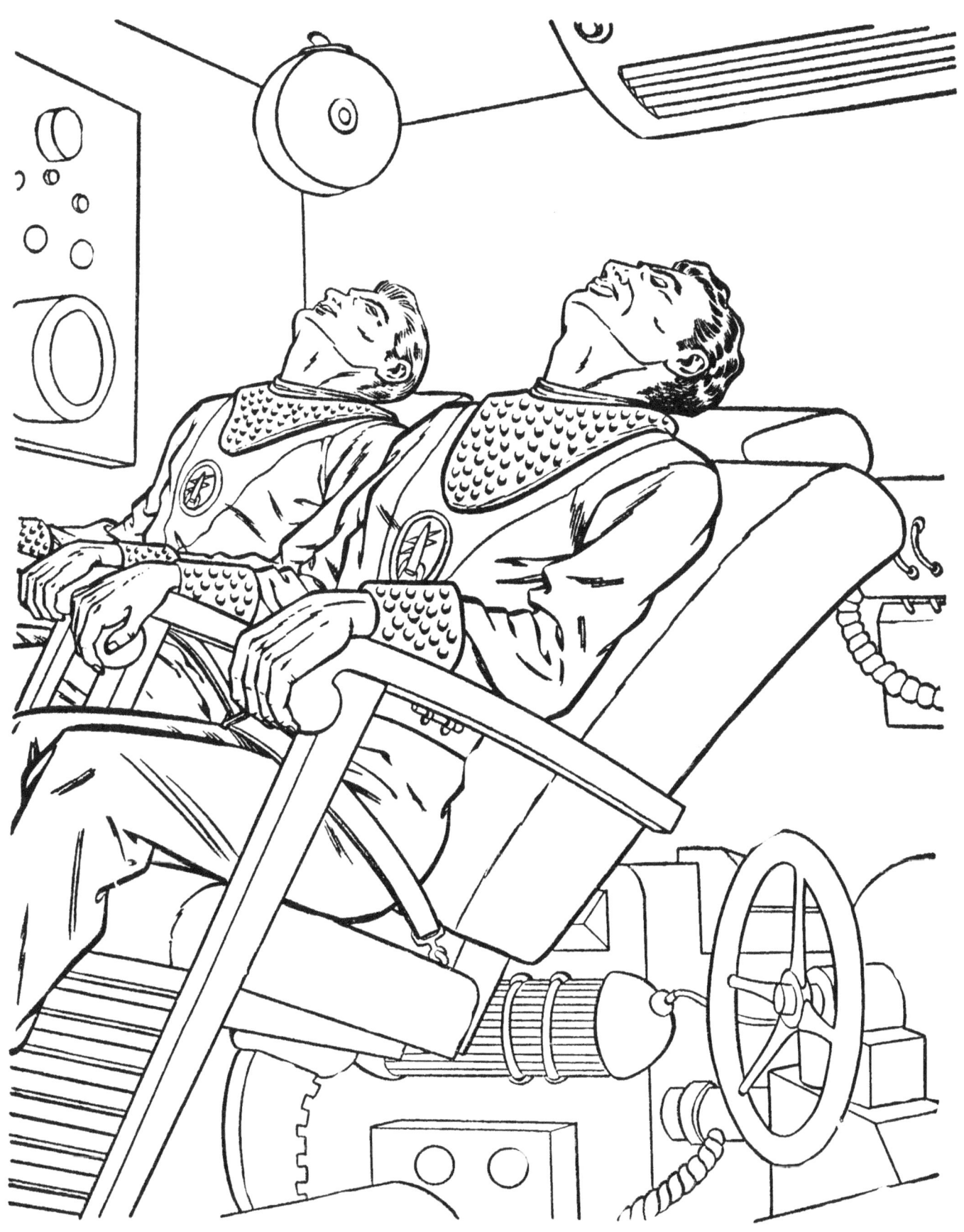

ACCELERATION!

BREAKING THROUGH THE ATMOSPHERE

A LITTLE FUN ABOARD SHIP

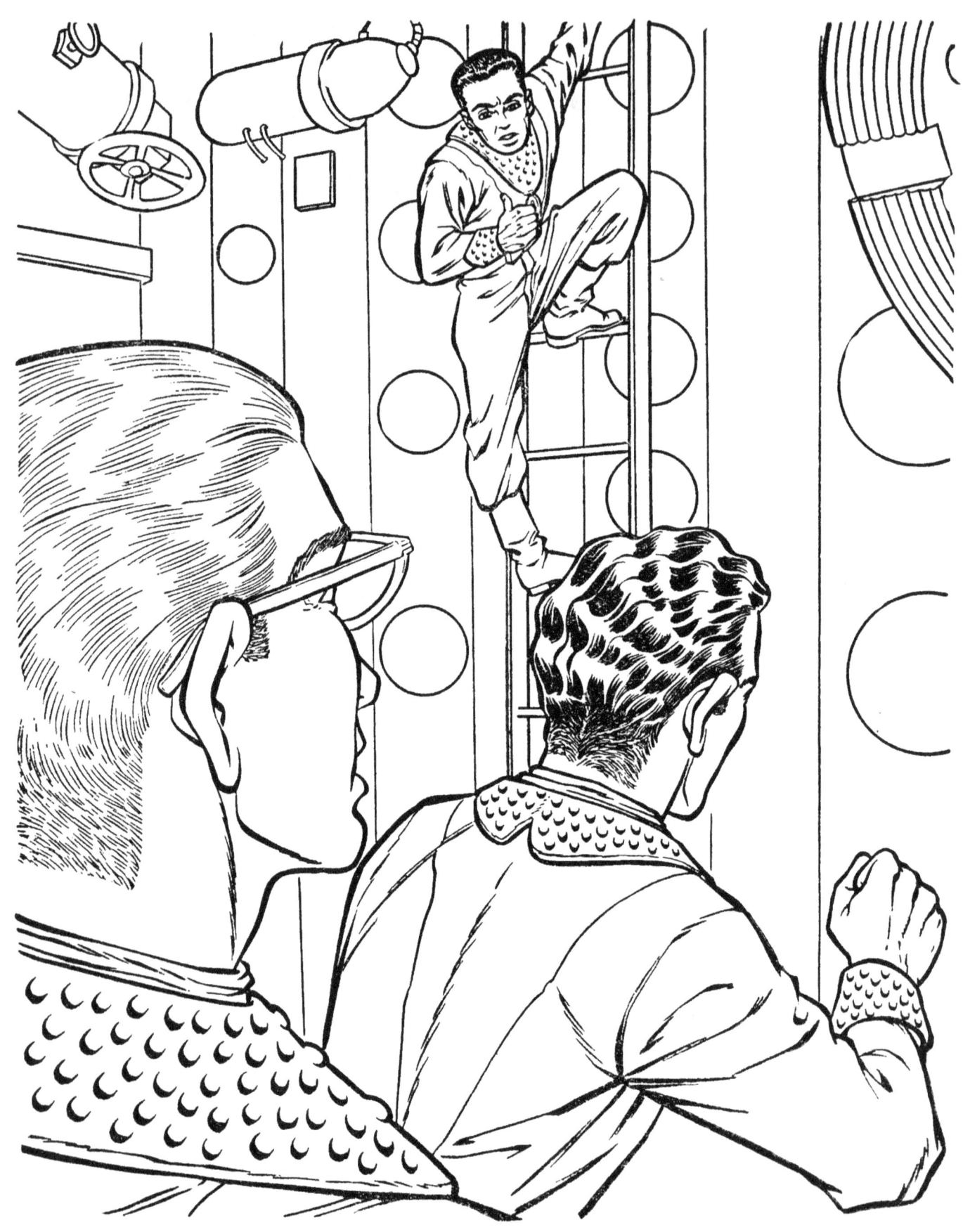

LOSING POWER

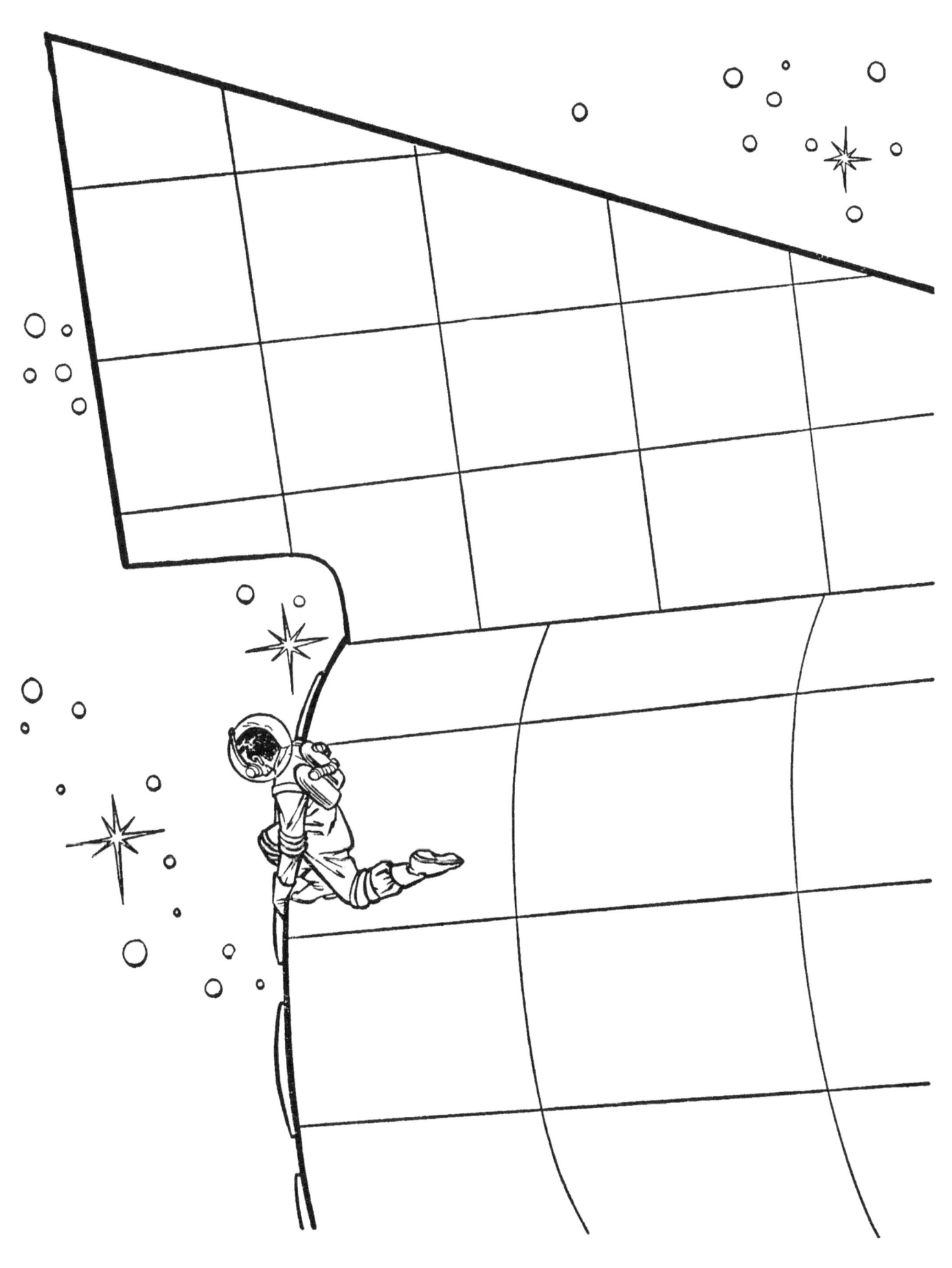

ASTRO INVESTIGATES

ROGER SUITS UP TO HELP

ALFY SPIES A SPACE PIRATE SHIP

PIRATE SHIP CLOSES IN

THE PIRATE BRINGS POLARIS INTO VIEW

Pirate captain orders super magnet energized

Astro ducks back into Polaris in a hurry

Joan Dale, Tom, and Astro try to escape from the pirates

Dr. Dale contacts base to warn of trouble

THE PIRATE SHIP FORCES POLARIS DOWN

The Polaris crew discusses the seemingly hopeless problem

Tom must get a message to land -- or else!

Tom deploys his crew to search for the pirates

WHILE SEARCHING, TOM HEARS A SCREAM

Back at the ship, Tom finds Dr. Dale in the clutch of a pirate

ROGER GOES INTO ACTION

TOM TACKLES THE SPACE PIRATE

THE PIRATE CAPTAIN IS ARRESTED BY TOM

As the pirate ship escapes, Manning yells, "The crew got away!"

Back in ship, the Polaris crew decides to continue the scientific mission, and let the Solar Guard take care of the pirates